Stormy

By Elizabeth Mills

Illustrated by Jacqueline Rogers

SCHOLASTIC INC.

New York Toronto London Auckland
Sydney Mexico City New Delhi Hong Kong

To Grace Maccarone–
You gave me my first writing project and believed in me as a writer.
I learned so much from you. Thank you.
–J. E. M.

For baby Abbey
–J. R.

For information regarding permissions, write to Scholastic Inc., Attention: Permissions Department, 557 Broadway, New York, NY 10012.

Library of Congress Cataloging-in-Publication Data is available.

ISBN 978-0-545-23409-2

10 9 8 7 6 5 4 3 2 1 10 11 12 13 14 15/0

Printed in the U.S.A. 40
This edition first printing, September 2010

Table of Contents

Rivals

Hannah and her black-and-white American Paint Horse, Casey, won many jumping classes.

Casey's stall was covered in blue ribbons.

In the practice ring at Shady Glen Stables, Casey's rich coat shone in the sun as he leaped over fences and cantered around the arena.

Hannah sat up straight in her saddle. She looked perfect on Casey. But when Hannah was not riding her horse, she walked around with her nose in the air.

"I'm the best rider at this stable," Hannah said.

"Just because you've won a lot of ribbons doesn't mean you're the best rider," said Becky.

Becky owned a chestnut Appaloosa mare named Stormy. Stormy was a good jumper and fun to ride. But there were

some fences that she was afraid to jump.

Stormy's stall had a few ribbons on it.

"Oh, yeah?" asked Hannah. "You've never won anything!"

"We'll see who wins at the next show," said Becky, "and then we'll know who's the best!"

“There’s a show in one month,” said Hannah. “Think you’ll be ready?”

“Stormy and I will be there,” said Becky. “And we’ll win!”

The next day, Becky practiced with Stormy.

"C'mon, girl, you can do it!" said Becky.

But Stormy would refuse to jump certain fences.

"What are we going to do, Stormy?" Becky said. "How are we ever going to beat Hannah if we can't get around the course?"

The Accident

Meanwhile, Hannah was showing off in the next ring.

"This jump is easy!" she said.

She and Casey trotted right up to the high jump and sailed over it. But Hannah's foot came out of her stirrup on the landing.

"OW!" said Hannah as she hit the ground. "My ankle!"

Her trainer ran right over.

"Ow, ow, ow!" Hannah said, holding her ankle.

"Let me see, Hannah," said the trainer.

“Your ankle is badly sprained, Hannah,” said the trainer. “I think you’re going to need a cast.”

“No, I’m okay!” said Hannah.

She tried to stand up. But she fell right over.

“Owwww! This isn’t fair!” she said, and she began to cry.

Becky and Stormy watched from the edge of the ring.

"If Hannah can't ride," Becky said to Stormy, "then maybe we have a chance!"

While the others followed Hannah into the barn, Becky and Stormy practiced jumping.

The next day, Hannah's ankle was in a walking cast. She hobbled around on crutches.

"Does it hurt?" asked one girl.

"How long will your leg be in a cast?" asked another.

"It does hurt," said Hannah, "and I have to wear the cast for four weeks!"

"Oh, no!" said a third girl. "You'll miss the competition!"

"I'm sad I can't ride," said Hannah. "What will Casey do without me?"

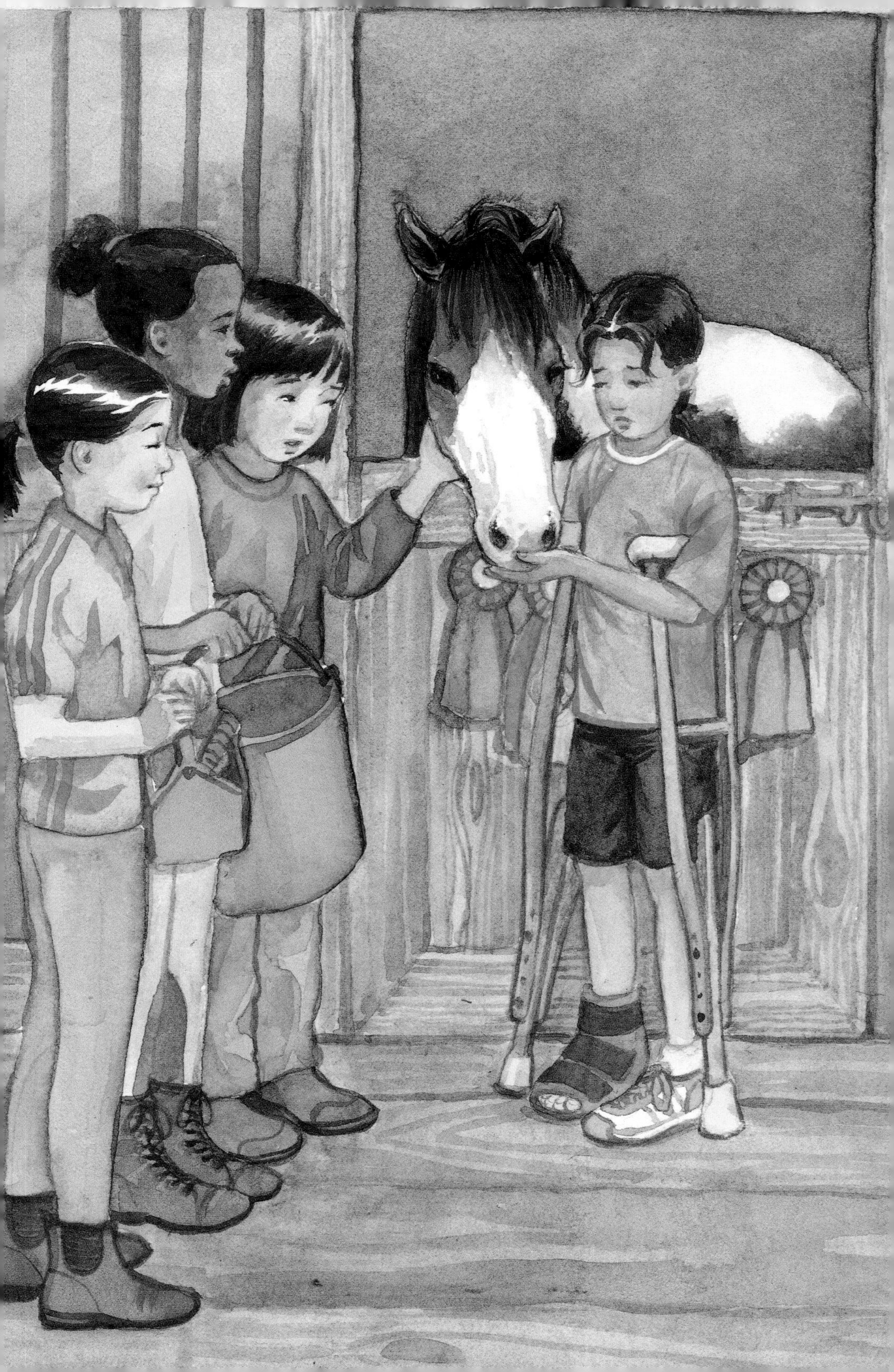

Chapter 3

Sticks and Stones

Inside the barn, Becky tacked up Stormy.

"We're going to have a great practice today," she told her horse. "Let's go!"

But Stormy would still not jump certain fences.

"What's wrong, Becky?" called Hannah from the fence. "Is your horse afraid? Or are you the 'fraidy-cat?"

"I'm not afraid!" Becky shouted.

Becky turned around and rode Stormy back to the fence with the yellow flower box and showed it to her quickly.

"Come on, girl," Becky said. "Let's try this jump again."

But Stormy would not go over the jump.

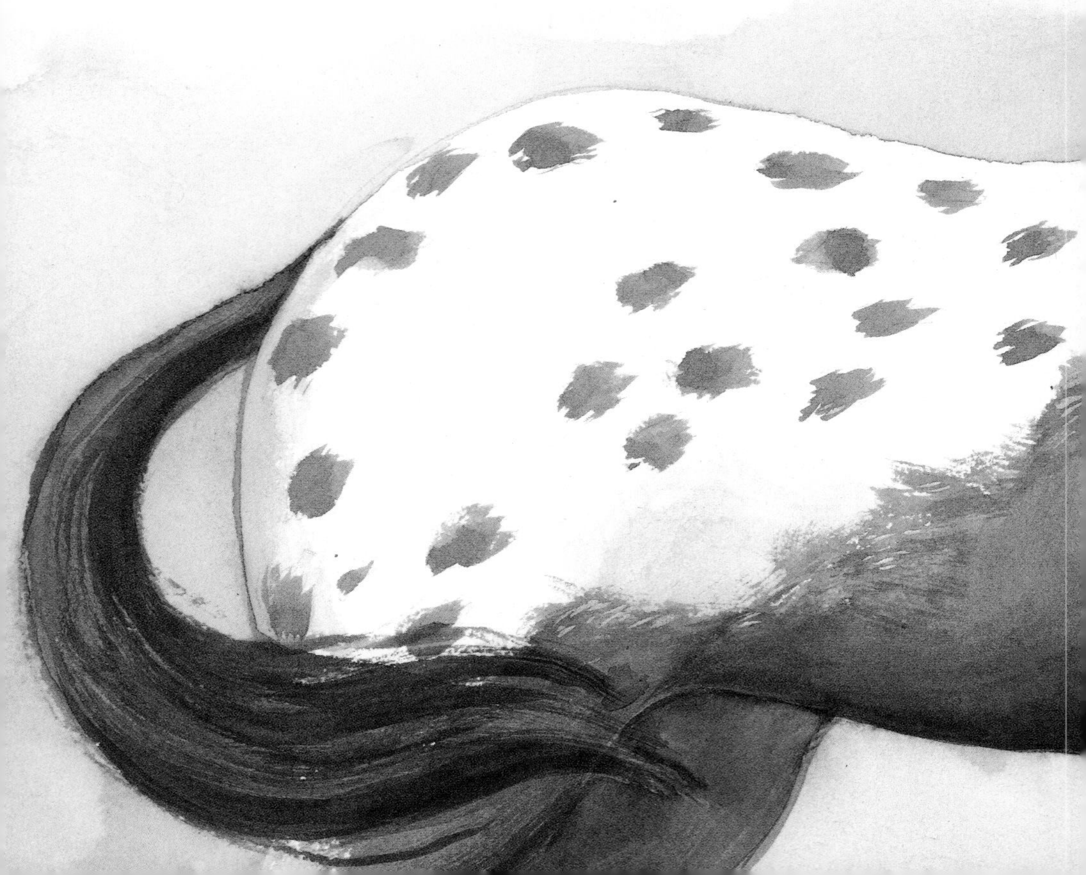

Becky dismounted and took her horse into the barn. She brushed Stormy and ran her hand over her back.

"Don't listen to her, girl. Somehow we're going to figure out how to get you over that fence and win that class at the show!"

The next few days were full of teasing from Hannah. She found something wrong with everything Becky did.

First Hannah thought Becky should spend more time showing Stormy the fences. Then she thought Becky was dropping her hands before she got to the fence. Becky tried to ignore Hannah, but it was too much.

One afternoon, Becky didn't see Hannah out at the ring. The practice went well, and Stormy jumped the entire course, even the fence with the yellow flower box!

"Good girl!" said Becky. "You're doing much better!"

Becky felt happy and relaxed.

After practice, Becky went into the barn and heard someone crying. She looked into the first stall, but no one was there. She looked into the next two stalls, but they were empty.

Then, at the back of the barn, she found Hannah in tears.

Chapter 4

Friends

"Hannah?" Becky asked. "What's wrong?"

"Go away!" said Hannah.

"Why are you crying?" asked Becky.

“I miss riding Casey so much,” said Hannah. “And now I have to watch you ride. It’s not fair!”

“But you’ve been teasing me,” Becky said. “You’ve been so mean. I thought you didn’t care about anything.”

Hannah burst into tears again. “I do care. I hate not being able to ride!” She hid her face.

Becky put her arm around Hannah.

"When you fell, I didn't check to make sure you were okay," Becky said. "I hoped that maybe you couldn't compete. All I cared about was winning. I'm sorry."

"I'm sorry, too," said Hannah. "I've been so stuck-up and mean to you. I was afraid you would become a better rider than me."

"I don't think I can be better than you," said Becky. "But I'd like to be as good as you. Would you help me? I think you might have been right about some of the things you said."

"Really?" asked Hannah. "Sure! We can start tomorrow." She wiped her eyes and sniffed loudly.

Becky helped Hannah to her feet and got her crutches.

"See you later, Hop-along Hannah," said Becky.

The next day, the two girls were at the ring together.

"Okay, Becky," said Hannah. "I think you need to show Stormy that fence and let her have a good long look at it. She needs to understand that the fence with the yellow flower box is just like any other fence."

When Becky rode over to the fence, Stormy snorted a little and tried to walk away.

“Why does she do that?” asked Becky.

“I don’t know,” said Hannah. “Maybe she fell at a fence like that once. Your job is to make sure she knows it won’t hurt her and after a while, she’ll forget about it and jump it every time.”

Becky took a deep breath, let it out, then circled around to start the course again. She led Stormy straight to the yellow-flower-box fence and Stormy cleared it perfectly!

"Great jump, girl!" said Becky.

"Yay!" said Hannah. "Now see if you can get her around the whole course."

But again Stormy stopped.

"Now what did I do?" asked Becky.

"You need to let Stormy know that she must go forward and jump every fence."

Becky and Stormy tried the course again. This time Becky was determined. She clucked and squeezed her legs very tight as she approached the fence, and Stormy sailed over it.

"All right!" said Hannah. "That's the way a winner rides!"

The girls continued to practice together. Becky and Stormy got better and learned to trust each other. And the girls became good friends, too. They joked and laughed and teased each other without ever being mean.

One day, Hannah came to the stables without her crutches.

"Hey, Hop-along Hannah!" said Becky. "Your cast is off early."

"Yes," said Hannah. "The doctor said I can start riding again! I'm so happy! But don't worry, I can't compete yet. The show is yours to win!"

"Do you think I can win?" asked Becky.

"I do!" said Hannah. "You're going to be great!"

On the day of the competition, Becky and Stormy flew over every jump and landed perfectly.

When the class was over, they won their first blue ribbon. Becky gave Hannah and Stormy a huge hug.

"Isn't it great being friends?" asked Hannah.

"Yes, it is!" said Becky.

And they laughed together.

About the Horses

Facts about Appaloosas:

© Lynn Stone/AgStock Images/Corbis

1. Appaloosas were originally bred in the American Northwest by the Nez Perce Indians.
2. Appaloosas are easy to find in a herd because of the pattern of color on their coats. But the term Appaloosa refers to a breed, not a color.
3. Appaloosas have very good endurance.
4. An average Appaloosa is usually between 14 and 16 hands high and weighs around 1,000 pounds.
5. The Appaloosa Horse Club recognizes five basic coat patterns: Leopard, Snowflake, Frost, Blanket, and Marble.

Facts about American Paint Horses:

© Kelly Funk/All Canada Photos/Getty Images

1. American Paint Horses are descended from Spanish horses that were brought to the United States hundreds of years ago.
2. The American Paint Horse Association is the second-largest breed registry in the United States.
3. Cowboys in the western plains liked Paints because they are strong and they work hard.
4. Paints are used for rodeos, trail riding, working on a ranch, and shows.
5. Paints and Pintos are related but not the same horse breed. Most Paints are also Pintos, but not all Pintos are Paints.

READ THEM ALL!
Every horse has a story.
BREYER Stablemates
Belle
Lucky
Patch
Penny
Starlight
Snowflake
Dash
Diamond
SCHOLASTIC
www.scholastic.com • www.breyerhorses.com